Lies and
Deception

Lies and
Deception

Debra Sallee

authorHOUSE®

AuthorHouse™
1663 Liberty Drive
Bloomington, IN 47403
www.authorhouse.com
Phone: 1-800-839-8640

Published by AuthorHouse   05/20/2013

ISBN: 978-1-4817-5600-6 (sc)
ISBN: 978-1-4817-5599-3 (e)

Library of Congress Control Number: 2013909414

CHAPTER 1

⟶∿∘ᴏ◟ᴏ⟋ᴏ◝ᴏ⟍ᴏ∿⟵

NATASHA CONRAD WAS JUST SITTING in her office, just wondering what she was going to do next.

Then next thing she sees is a very handsome man standing in the doorway of her office, she said, may I help you, he said, are you Natasha Conrad private investigator, my name is John Clark and I wanted to know if you could help me find my brother.

Natasha told him to come in and have a seat, do you have any information about your brother. He told her that they were from Vermont and his brother Jack Clark just vanished.

She said, do you have any idea where he's at now, John said, the last I knew he was right here in Texas.

1

Natasha said, I will help you find your brother, my fee three hundred a day and all expenses. I will start tomorrow, can you tell me anything else.

She said, do you have a picture of him, John said yes, I have one with me, so he gave it to her an she looked at it, she said, you guys look like twins, John said, we are.

It was time for Natasha's office to close, so she closed and went home. She got home and realized she was hungry and left her apartment to go get something to eat.

She was really hungry for a nice juicy steak, so she found a nice quiet place on the out skirts of town she walked in, took a table and placed her order, steak, bake potato, corn on the cob, and salad.

She was sitting there eating enjoying her food, she looked up from her plate and John Clark walked in, he seen her and she asked him to sit at the table with her, so he sat down.

They ate there dinner, then after they started talking about his brother Jack, how did he just vanish without a trace, when he got old enough he just up and left in the middle of the night and we haven't seen him since, whose we? Me and my mother, where is your father? Oh he's never been there for us. I guess my mom told me that my dad would only come to Vermont sometimes.

Natasha spoke up and said, that her parents owned a cabin in Vermont and they would only go up on weekends or my dad would go just to get away

Natasha and John finished their talk and Natasha told John she would see him tomorrow around 9:00 o'clock am. Then she went home. She got back to her apartment locked the door and went into take a shower.

John arrived at the hotel where he is staying until he can find his brother, he went up to his room dropped his keys on the table and decided he would take a shower and go to bed.

John got up the next morning called room service for coffee and breakfast he ate his breakfast and decided to get dressed. He wore blue jeans and a t-shirt, than headed down to get in his truck and head to Natasha's office.

He got to her office but she wasn't there yet so he waited in her office. Ten minutes later Natasha showed up, she had a cup of coffee for her and John.

Natasha said, where do us two start, John said, why don't we go to the police station and see if they have anything on my brother. Natasha said, I have a friend down at the station I could call to have him check for me.

She made the call to her friend at the station, Chuck Mooney, Chuck said, well hello, Natasha it's been a long time, what can I do for you? She said, I need you to look up a name for me and see if you can find out anything on him, his name, Jack Clark then let me know. Please.

John said, lets go down to the DMV and see if he's got a driver's license, she says yeah, we can try, but I don't know if they will tell us anything.

Liz Conrad, Natasha's mom was just sitting in her cabin in Vermont, she was thinking about calling Natasha at her apartment, but figured she would still be at work so she called her their.

She had called and the secretary Marie Adams answered the phone, Hello Conrad Investigations how may I help you, hello Marie this is Liz Conrad is my daughter in? Marie says, sorry Mrs. Conrad you missed her, okay just tell her that her mother called.

Liz just didn't know what to do about the dream she'd been having about Natasha's dad, it just didn't make any sense to her.

She just had to talk to her daughter about it to see if they could make any sense out of it, she's wondering why now, my husband has been gone for 5 years.

Natasha and John went down to the DMV she asked them if they had anything about a drivers license for a Jack Clark. The lady behind the counter said, we have a Jack Clark listed for a license 4 years ago, John and Natasha said, thank you then they left. John asked Natasha now what do we do, he hasn't got a drivers license in 4 years, I was hoping to come out with some address or something. They headed back to her office when they got there Marie was on the phone, when she got done, she went and knocked on the door Natasha said, come in, Marie said, here's your messages and one of them is from your mom.

Natasha asked Marie did she say what she wanted and Marie said no, she just said, just tell her I called. Natasha was wondering what her mom wanted, so she told John do you mind and John said no. So she called her mom and there was no answer, so she said, I'll call her later.

Chuck Mooney was into this investigation about some art smugglers at the art center, he went down to the art center and talk to the manager of the center and the security people. They have a very high tech security system, so who ever done this knew what They were doing.

Detective Mooney looked around but didn't touch anything until the CSI were done with gathering evidences. Mooney just said, who ever did this knew what they were doing getting around the alarm system they just came in got what they wanted and left, so who ever it was came into the center and case the place first.

Natasha told John there isn't much more we can do today, so if you want to come back tomorrow about 9:00 o'clock am we can get started again. So John left and Natasha told her secretary to go home she would see her tomorrow. Then Natasha stayed at the office for about a half hour looking over some paper work, then just remember she has to call Chuck Mooney tomorrow when she came in to see if he had anything on Jack Clark.

So she left the office went to her car and decided she would stop and get her some Chinese for dinner, so she wouldn't have to worry about fixing dinner, when she gets home. She got home came in threw her keys on the table and got her a fork so she could eat her Chinese.

She ate, took a shower, then watched some TV and then went to bed.

CHAPTER 2

—⁓∘◦◦❦❦◦◦⁓—

NATASHA GOT UP AND CALLED her mother, her mom picked it up on the third ring, hello mom how are you doing? Fine except for the dreams I've been having about your father, what dreams about dad? That's why I called your office yesterday to talk to you about the dreams.

How do they start out? Well all it is, is your dad is saying is help Natasha find, find what mom? I don't know what all he says is help Natasha find and the dream is over. So mom what are you suppose to help me find? I don't know darling, but I guess we will soon find out.

Okay mom I have to get ready and go to work, but if you have anymore dreams just let me know and we will piece this together, I love you mom.

Natasha got her shower ate her breakfast, then went out and got in her car and went to work.

Marie was at work already she made coffee and had a basket of muffins for her and Natasha. Natasha got to work an as she was going to her office she asked Marie if there was any coffee and she said, it was brewing right now. Marie asked Natasha is your mom alright? Yeah, it was about a dream she's been having about my dad, it's just telling her she has to help me find and that's the end there's no more.

It was 9:00 o'clock and here comes John, Marie told him to go ahead and go in she is waiting for you. So John went right in and Natasha asked him if he would like some coffee and a muffin and he said, yeah.

So John says what is our plans for today, she said, first I am going to call my friend Chuck and see if he has anything on your brother, so she called Chuck and he answered on the second ring, hello detective Mooney, hello Chuck this is Natasha have you any information for me about Jack Clark.

Chuck said, I haven't got to it yet I've been working on this art smuggling case, how's that going for you? I just want to know how they disarmed a high tech security system. I'm sure these guys that did it have a boss, but I just don't know who. But Natasha if I find out anything about your guy I'll let you know, okay Chuck thanks. John said, so how are we going to find my brother. Natasha said John is there anything else you can tell me? Well Jack use to draw as he was growing up and use to love to go to the art museum and look at the art there, I remember him saying, he's going to have art like that some day. And we made a pat when we were old enough that we would get each others name tattooed on our arms, he put my name on his arm and I got his name on my arm, that way we would always be together.

Natasha says wait a minute John, you said Jack was into art, yeah! So, we just might of got a connection, what do you mean, my friend Chuck just told me he is working on this art smuggling case and he said, whoever did it was doing it for there boss, but he don't know who the boss is. And you think it might be Jack, it's a shot, let's go down and talk to Chuck, let me call him first to see if he can see us.

Natasha called Chuck at the station, hello detective Mooney, hay Chuck this is Natasha again, first let me tell you that I'm working on this case and I think it might have to do with your case, so do you have time to talk? Yeah, come on down.

Natasha and John went down to the station to talk to Chuck. Chuck said, come on in, so they went into his office an sat down, Natasha introduced John to Chuck, this is my case John Clark hired me to look for his brother, to make a long story short, we think the guy you are looking for is John's brother Jack.

Chuck said, what makes you think that? Then John said, my brother and me use to go to art museums and look at the art an one day he told me he would have art like that someday.

If he is the man I'm looking for how can I truly be sure that it's him? Well John said, one we our twins and another if it's him he has my name tattooed on his arm, just like I got his name on my arm. Chuck said, I will have to see what I can dig up on your brother, will you please let us know. Oh Chuck we also went down to the DMV and he hasn't got a drivers license in 4 years.

Natasha and John went back to her office and went over the case so far, they didn't ave much but they would wait and see what Chuck came up with. Then Natasha told John that was it for the day and she would see him tomorrow. Natasha left and went down an got in her car and went home. She decided she would take a shower then get her something to eat and then she would call her mother.

Natasha called her mom and she picked up on the second ring, hi mom, have anymore dreams about dad? No Natasha still the same one, well let me know if it changes, oh mom by the way what are you doing at the cabin? I thought I'd get away for awhile I haven't been up here since your dad past away.

Natasha asked her mom, do you want me to come up to the cabin this weekend an stay with you? That would be nice, we really haven't spent no time together, okay I will see you Friday night love you mom, love you to Natasha.

John was heading back to his hotel, when he decided he would stop and get something to eat and take back to his room, so that way he wouldn't have to call room service.

He got back to his room and sat an ate his Chinese food, then the phone rang in his room, hello John, this is Natasha I thought I'd let you know I am going to be out of town on Friday, I'm going to Vermont to the family cabin to spend the weekend with my mom, John said okay when are you leaving? Friday morning, I'm sure if you have any questions just call and ask for Chuck.

I will see you tomorrow right? Yeah! We'll see if Chuck has anything and will go from there.

Liz was sitting outside on her back deck at the cabin just trying to figure out her dream, and why she hasn't got no more information then what she's already got, she keeps asking herself what she's got to help Natasha find, she just didn't know what her husband was trying to tell her.

Natasha got up the next morning to go to the office and figured she was going to go get breakfast first. She got to the diner an sat at a corner table an grabbed the menu to see what she wanted, she ordered scrambled eggs, toast, bacon and a coffee, she ate her breakfast, just thinking about the day an the weekend. She got done eating and left to go to the office. She sat there waiting for John, hoping she would find out something from Chuck. John showed up and he said so are we going to call Chuck and see if he found out anything.

Natasha called Chuck hello Chuck, so have you found out anything? Yeah, I found out that he had his last driver license 4 years ago, I checked the last address listed for him, but it didn't pan out. Natasha I'm sorry

I don't have much for you but I will keep trying to find out something, well thank you, Chuck spoke up and ask Natasha what she was going to be doing after work, she said, well I'm going to be packing to go to Vermont tomorrow, she said, why? Would you like to go to dinner before you go home an pack, let me close up the office an go home and freshen up and I'll call you and you can come to my apartment and I'll cook dinner for you. That sounds good, I'll see you later goodbye.

CHAPTER 3

————ᴡᴡᴇᴏᴏᴇᴛᴏᴏᴇᴇᴏᴏᴡᴡ————

So Natasha phoned Chuck and said, okay I'm going to be cooking dinner for us, I'll see you later, Chuck got ready to go to Natasha's for dinner, he put on a t-shirt and jeans an boots and he was ready to go, so he went out an got in his truck and left.

Natasha was cooking dinner when Chuck got there, Chuck knocked on the door an she let him in he had flowers in his hand for her, he handed them to her and she said, thank you. She was making some Mexican dish she seen her mother make an Chuck said, that smells good.

She was almost done packing and Chuck said, what time do you get your plane? She said, around 7:00 o'clock tomorrow morning, I should be in Vermont on Friday around noon. Do you need me to take you to the airport?

That would be nice. So they ate there dinner with a bottle of wine and talked awhile and then Chuck helped her clean up the kitchen and then went into the living room and finished there wine.

Natasha told Chuck I told John Clark if he wanted to know anything new he could get a hold of you and I also gave him my number in Vermont. Chuck said, okay, but you know what if his brother is behind this why hasn't he been caught yet? Natasha said, well we know he's keeping a low profile, because he has other guys doing the dirty work for him, he just sets it up, make the plan of how it's all got to be done, that's why he hasn't been caught yet.

Chuck said, I think I'll be going now so you can get some sleep, and I will be here at 5:30 tomorrow morning to pick you up, okay that sounds good, so she walked him to the door, and Chuck looked up to say something to her and he just kissed her, he said, oh! I'm so sorry I should of asked first, she said that's alright I wanted it just as bad as you.

Chuck left an Natasha just stood there for a minute in a trans, thinking that was just a kiss and it's been a long time coming, she's known Chuck since she started her PI office, so it wasn't like they were strangers.

Natasha went to her room to make sure she had everything she was going to need in Vermont. She figured she'd call her mom and let her know what time she'd be there. Her mom answered the phone Natasha said, hi, I thought I'd let you know when I would get into Vermont, well I leave at 7:00 o'clock tomorrow morning and won't get into Vermont until Friday at noon, I will rent a car at the airport and drive up to the cabin so I will see you when I get there. Have you had anymore dreams than what you've already told me? No, still just the same information I gave you already. Okay mom I will see you Friday.

John was sitting in his hotel room wondering if Natasha had told Chuck, so he decided, he would call Chuck, so he dialed Chuck's cell phone, an Chuck picked it up an said, Chuck this is John Clark, I was wondering if you know that Natasha is going to Vermont an she told me if I have any questions I could talk to you? Yeah! But right now I don't have anything, because it's like they stopped there break-ins for awhile, okay.

Chuck spoke up and said yes I know Natasha's is going to Vermont, because we had dinner tonight and I am taking her to the airport tomorrow morning.

Liz is standing at the window of her cabin, thinking it's going to be nice having Natasha here for the weekend, because she hasn't really been up here since her father's death. So Liz figured she would be up for awhile she would get the spare room all cleaned up and get it ready for Natasha's arrival.

Natasha got up the next morning she made coffee and while the coffee was making she figured she would take a shower and get dressed and get ready, so when Chuck showed up she would be ready to go.

So she took her shower, then she decided she would wear slacks, a nice dress top and a pair of nice shoes.

Then there was a knock on her door she opened it, it was Chuck she told him there was coffee and muffins in the kitchen help himself.

He said are you excited about going to the cabin and seeing your mother? She said. Yeah, kind of I haven't been to the cabin since my dad's death, but my moms having some dreams and we our hoping to find out what they mean.

Natasha told Chuck if you find out anything about Jack Clark or if he's connected to your case please call me on my cell phone. He said okay and I will let John know too.

Chuck asked her if she was ready to go to the airport an she said yes, so she got her purse, keys and made sure everything was shut off, an he grabbed her suitcase an they were on there way.

She was a little nervous and he said why you nervous? She says because I haven't been here in 5 years and it kind of scares me, he grabbed her hand and told her she would be fine an if she needed someone to talk to she could call him anytime

They got to the airport an he pulled right up to the door, an before she got out he turned her chin towards him and he told her you will be fine and then he kissed her an she, kissed him back an told him thank you an I want you to know I love you an I've always have ever since I met you for the first time.

CHAPTER 4

—⌇⌇◦◦◦◦◦◦⌇⌇—

SHE GOT OFF THE PLANE and went to get her bag and then went to see about renting a car.

She got her rented car, put her bag in the trunk and was on her way to the cabin. Natasha thought it was going to be strange being there since she hasn't been there since her father died.

She was going down the highway and her cell phone rang so she pulled along the road too answer her phone it was Chuck, hello Chuck I was calling to see if your plane landed alright? Yeah, I'm on my way to the cabin. Well I will call you later and Natasha I love you too.

Natasha hung up and started down the highway again, just driving looking at some new changes since she was here last. She finally got to her exit and turned off she was really going to be happy to see her mom.

Liz was just doing some last minute touch-ups before her daughter got there she was kind of excited that Natasha was coming since she hasn't been here in 5 years, it was going to be strange for the both of them but they would be fine.

John Clark figured he wouldn't find out much this weekend so he figured he would go to Vermont and visit his mother, so he packed his bags and went to the airport, got his ticket and waited for his flight to leave.

Chuck figured there wasn't much happening today so he was going to go home and wait for Natasha to call so he left. He got home and he threw his keys on the counter and headed for the shower.

Natasha finally got to the cabin and she sat in the car for a minute taking in all the beautiful flowers, the lovely landscaping, it was just something she has never seen before. She got out of the car and her mother came out to meet her, Liz says, good afternoon baby and they hugged and kissed each others cheek.

Mom the flowers and the landscaping is outstanding, it is just nothing like I've ever seen, oh, I have a person who takes care of the place when I'm not here and he does a very good job. Liz says come on in I've got ice tea waiting for us. They sat down and drank there tea and Natasha said, anymore dreams mom? No, it just doesn't make sense, well hopefully we will find out what or who we our looking to find. Natasha said mom I'm going to get my bag out of the car and then we can get more ice tea and go sit on the deck.

Chuck was sitting at home thinking about Natasha and how he missed her already then his phone rang, there was a silent alarm going off at a art gallery, he put on his boots got

In his truck an was gone. He got to the art gallery first and went inside the security guard met him at the door, Chuck said, you stay put, I will go in and when he got to all the expensive painting there he saw two men dressed in black, stealing painting's, he told them to freeze and they dropped everything and Chuck went up to them an handcuffed them an waited for back-up.

When back-up showed up he read them there rights and then started asking them questions, he showed them Jack Clark's picture is this the guy your working for, they said, they didn't know because they never seen him, all they know is they do the job and take the paintings or art to another place an someone else comes an gets them, but its not that guy. So they arrested them and took them to jail, where they would be questioning them again

Liz and Natasha were sipping there ice tea an looking at scenery an talking, Natasha said, so mom no more dreams since the last? Liz said, nothing is different maybe we'll learn something else tonight. Mom what do you want for dinner or do you want to go out to eat I'm buying. Well Natasha I thought we could eat here we both will make dinner.

So John's flight was being called and he gave them his ticket an he boarded the plane, he found his seat, he figured he wouldn't call his mom he would surprise her.

CHAPTER 5

—⁓ₒₐₑₜₒₒₜₑₒₒₘ—

CHUCK QUESTIONED THE TWO GUYS he arrested okay guys who do you work for? The guys said, like I said we take it to another place and someone else picks it up, or if this guy works for the same one we do.

So right now gentlemen you guys are the ones who are going to jail for the robbery, and did you guys do the art center robbery too? They said yes, but it's the same thing as this robbery

Natasha and her mom made chicken and noodles, bread sticks, and salad, they ate there dinner and cleaned the kitchen an then went in an watched TV, then it came over the TV about the robbery at the art gallery and Natasha wanted to know if Chuck was the detective on the case, then the reporter came on an said that Detective Chuck Mooney was the arresting officer. So Natasha called his cell phone and she got his voice mail, so she left a message to call her back.

John landed at the airport went to get his bag and went to see if he could rent a car, he got his car put his bag in the trunk an headed down the highway, and hoping when he got there his mom would be home.

Chuck got Natasha's voice mail message and called her back, her phone rang and she answered it on the second ring, hello, Chuck is that you? Yes I just got your message, I heard on the TV about the robbery did you get them? Yes I did, they didn't know about the silent alarm, so when I got to the gallery I caught them in the act. You okay? Yes I handcuffed them and waited for back-up. Natasha how is everything going with your mom? No new dreams but hopefully we will find out more tonight, Chuck I was worried about you, I'm fine, well I will talk to you tomorrow okay I love you bye.

John finally got to his mom's house and he pulled in the driveway and his mom is standing at the window an when he got out of the car his mom went to the door and ran out to meet her son, he said, how have you been? She said fine, have you heard from Jack, she said no, they went into the house and sat down an had a glass of lemonade, an started talking about Jack. John said, mom I've been in Texas, hired a PI and she is good we haven't found out anything yet but I will keep looking. Then John asked his mom, where is my father? His mother said, John your dad is gone, he died about five years ago, mom what is his name, John right now that is not important, why? Because John he was a married man and he had a daughter and wife. So other words I have a half sister out there somewhere.

That hit John like a club, then he told his mom, not only am I looking for my brother, now I have a half sister to find, then he went to his car and got his bag out of the trunk.

John went inside and told his mom my old room? She said, yeah! He went up and put his bag in his room and stop an looked at himself in the mirror, sinking all this information in his head, he went back downstairs and found his mom sitting on the deck crying, he said, what's the matter? She said I'm sorry John I should have told you and Jack along time ago, that's alright mom I know now. Mom come on we are going out to eat.

Natasha said, mom I'm tried I think I am going to bed, her mom said I'm going too. I love you, mom. She went to her room an got her sweat pants and a t-shirt out to put on after she gets out of the shower, she took her shower dried off and had her hair up in a towel, she came back into her room got her sweat pants and t-shirt on took her hair out of the towel an brushed it and went to bed an went to sleep.

CHAPTER 6

$\sim\!\!\sim\!\!\sim\!\!\sim\!\!\sim\!\!\sim$

CHUCK WOKE UP THE NEXT morning figured he'd get some coffee and go down to the station and try to piece all this together an maybe talk to his two suspects again to see if he can find out anything else.

John got up the next morning and went downstairs to get coffee his mother was already up sitting at the table, so he got his coffee and sat at the table too. I'm going to call Natasha the PI I hired to find my brother to see if she can help me find my half sister too, John do you think she will find both of them? I think she will when I tell her the story.

Natasha got up and went to get some coffee, she went into the kitchen and her mom was at the stove cooking breakfast for them she said do you want some eggs and bacon, toast? Yeah, that sounds good, Natasha says mom did you have another dream last night? Liz said no nothing, Natasha said mom I had the dream this time, it really didn't make any sense, all dad said was that if we couldn't find it, it will find me, mom what will find me? It doesn't make sense and it's got me puzzled.

Then Natasha's cell phone went off, she went to answer it, she said, hello, Natasha this is John are you busy she said no I'm just getting ready to eat breakfast why, I need to talk to you it's important, can I call you back when I'm done eating? Yeah! Please Natasha call me back like I said it's important, okay later.

Chuck got down to the station went to his desk and sat down figured out what he was going to do, he called down to have them bring up his two suspects, they brought them up an put them in a room so Chuck could talk to them.

He came into the room and sat down in front of both of them, he said I know what you guys told me before, but is their anything else you can tell me about this guy you work for like we told you we never seen him, then how do you get your orders, he calls us from a pay phone to our cell phone and gives us our orders, but apparently he didn't know about the silent alarm at the art gallery, that's what gave you guys away and do you know what he does with all this art when he gets it, no all we do is deliver the art and leave it and somebody else picks it up for him, well who is this guy you leave the art with, I think he said his name is Tom Stevens, are you sure that's what he said? Yeah! Do you have a address for this guy? No, okay guys this is all you can tell me? Yeah.

So Chuck went out of the room and told the officers outside the room take them back to there cell.

So Natasha got done eating she called John back on his cell phone, hello, John this is Natasha, what's so important well Natasha where do I start, well I come to Vermont to visit my mom, so your in Vermont? Yes, would you like to meet somewhere to talk?

Yeah we'll go for coffee, that sounds good where do you want to meet a little café as you come into town, okay I will be there in about one hour okay.

Chuck picked up his cell phone and dialed Natasha's number, she picked it up on the second ring, hello Chuck what you doing? Just called to see how everything is going, it's going fine, no new dreams, I'm getting ready to go meet John he said he had something important to tell me, so we our meeting at the café in town for coffee, John's in Vermont? Yeah, he's here visiting his mother okay. I will talk to you later oh Chuck how bout we get together Monday night maybe go to dinner or something.

Natasha hung up and went an got her purse and keys to go an meet John, she got on the road and got to where she was suppose to meet him at the café. She walked in and John was sitting at a table so she sat down and they ordered coffee. John told Natasha that

When he got to his mother's he asked her, where my dad was and she told me that he was gone, he died about 5 years ago, I asked her what his name was and she told me that it wasn't important right now and I said why, and she told me that he was married and had a daughter, so not only do I have a brother to look for but I have a half sister to look for too, so I was wondering if you can help me find her. John do you know what your dad looks like I've only seen him a couple of times, do you have a picture of him, no he wouldn't let us take his picture, probably because he was married.

Yeah! John I will help you so we have to get back to Texas so we can get started. John I am leaving tomorrow at 7:00 pm so o wont be home until Monday at noon, okay how bout I leave at 7:00 pm and we can talk on the plane and then we can go to the office an get started? Okay, John then I am going to finish my coffee and go back to the cabin and I will see you at the airport.

Natasha got home and called Chuck hello Chuck, Natasha I thought I would call you and let you know that me and John are leaving at 7:00 pm tomorrow night and we would get into Texas at about noon, then we our going to my office, because John told me, that he found out from his mom that he has a half sister so he asked for my help. Okay Natasha I will see you Monday.

CHAPTER 7

—⁓◦◦◦◦◦◦◦—

NATASHA CALLED HER SECRETARY MARIE and Marie said, hello, Marie this is Natasha me and John will be back at noon on Monday oh! John is with you no he is at his mom's he called me and asked me to meet him for coffee, because he had to tell me something important. So I thought I'd let you know and I will see you Monday.

Liz was in the kitchen cooking something for lunch Natasha what's wrong, mom remember me telling you about this guy John I am working for to find his brother, will mom now he found out that he has a half sister too, how'd he find this out, his mom told him, he is just in shock, he can't believe all this is happening. Look at all the problems you're having finding his brother, is he hoping to find both of them. Natasha said, mom tonight we our going out for dinner my treat.

John went back to his mom's and she was sitting in the kitchen, mom what are you doing? Nothing John, just thinking how I really screwed things up for you and Jack, you guys just find your half sister, she has a right to know that she has brothers.

Chuck sat at his desk looking to punch in the name of this guy Tom Stevens to see if he can find an address or number, so he can go talk to him. So he punched in the name and all he got was an address so he wrote it down and he'll go check him out to see what he knows.

It was getting to be dinner time and Natasha asked her mom if she was ready to go and get something to eat, so she could get back to pack to catch her plane tomorrow afternoon. She asked her mom what she wanted to eat she said she didn't care, so they went to get Chinese, they got to the restaurant and took a seat by the window, ordered ice tea and waited to order there food. They ordered and waited for there food and Natasha told her mom, if you have anymore dreams or I do we let each other know.

John told his mom he was going to be upstairs packing his bag an she could let him know when it was time to eat dinner. John said, mom I don't blame you it's just something that happened mom I do remember a lot. I just wonder what my half sister is like and if she looks like me and Jack. Mom I am glad that you finally told me about my dad and my half sister.

Chuck got to the address of Ton Stevens knocked on the door and Tom answered the door. Tom Stevens, I'm detective Mooney can I ask you some questions about the robbery's of the art gallery and the art center, sure come on in have a seat. You know I could arrest you for receiving stolen property, hay look I just took the art from the two guys that did the robbery's then I'm to take the art to another location an then leave, you never stayed around to see who was picking it up.

Natasha got up bright and early Sunday morning she took a shower, got dressed an went downstairs to the kitchen where her mom was making her breakfast, so how's it going this morning? Fine no more dreams if that's what you're saying. Mom when I get to my office on Monday I will call you, I and John are going to the office after we get in on Monday. We're going there to see what we can figure out about his brother and half sister.

John got up took a shower got dressed and went to the kitchen, his mom asked him if he wanted some breakfast and he said no, just coffee, I have to meet Natasha at the airport so we can catch our flight back to Texas.

Chuck got to the station was just sitting there drinking coffee an figured he'd call Natasha to see if she was up so he called an she answered hello Natasha I was wondering if you were up yeah! Just waiting to leave to go catch my flight, so I will see you Monday? Yeah, okay talk to you later.

John and Natasha met at the airport to catch there flight back to Texas, they set next to each other on the flight an started talking about where they were going to start first, to see if they could find either one of them, his brother or sister.

CHAPTER 8

———ᴡᴏᴄᴇᴛᴏᴏᴛᴇᴏᴏᴡ———

CHUCK STILL DIDN'T KNOW WHO was behind the robberies of the art gallery and art center, and the guys who did the crime he had them in jail he just didn't know who the master mind was.

Chuck looked at his watch thinking well Natasha is on her way back home an he would see her when she gets here, he just was wondering how he fell in love so fast for Natasha, a very smart, very bright, very pretty, an he would so much like to take her to bed an make love to her.

But he didn't want to fill like he was rushing her he wanted her to be ready just like he is, because he cares very deeply for Natasha and respects her very much.

Marie got up to go into work Monday, she figured she would stop and buy some muffins and some donuts to take into the office. She also figured she would make some coffee and sit and eat a muffin or donut since the morning was going to be slow. Marie got to the office and it was very quiet she couldn't stand it so she turned on the radio and figured she would listen to some music

Liz figured she would get ready to pack and head back home to Maine, so it wasn't to late when she got home, she made a list out for the gardener of things she needed done while she was gone back home and she also left him money for everything he's done already, so she went up to her room and packed her bags.

John and Natasha got to the airport got their bags and went to John's truck and they headed for Natasha's office, Natasha told John I'll call Chuck when we get to the office to see if he has anything on Jack. They got to Natasha's office and Marie was sitting at her desk, Natasha said, any messages Marie no, so they went into her office and she sat at her desk an she ask John to sit, she said, so John what else can you tell me about your half sister, not very much, do you know what your dad's name is no, my mom never told me what his name was, she just told me he died 5 years ago. Plus she told me right now his name wasn't important, because he is a married man and has a wife and daughter. So have you ever seen your dad before when he came to visit you and Jack an your mom? Yeah, I kind of remember what he looks like if I see a picture of him. Okay John go home and I will talk to you tomorrow.

Natasha was sitting at her desk an decided to call Chuck, Chuck answered on the second ring, hello

Natasha so your home, Chuck how about coming to my place for dinner tonight around seven o'clock, oh an you can bring the wine, okay I will be there, oh it's nice to have you back Natasha.

John got back to his hotel room, ordered dinner, while he was waiting he unpacked his bag and took a shower and got relaxed and waited for his dinner, he read his mail, then there was a knock on the door, it was his dinner he ate dinner an watched some television an went over and over in his mind about his brother and half sister.

Natasha told Marie she was going to leave for the day because she had to unpack and she was having a guest for dinner, Marie says Natasha I don't mean to be nosy, but how is it going between you and Chuck? How do you know about me and Chuck, I can see how you too look at each other. Marie says I'm just happy for you and I hope you get something out of this relationship I just don't want you to get hurt. Natasha said, Marie Chuck is a very responsible person, very caring, handsome and very understanding.

So Natasha told Marie I am going home now, and when you finish what you are doing you can go home. See you tomorrow.

Liz got back to Maine so she figured she would call Natasha on her cell phone, Natasha answered on the second ring, hello mom, I was just leaving the office and I'm heading home to unpack and I have a guest coming for dinner is he a nice guy? Yes mom very nice and handsome, what can I do for you mom, I just thought I would call and see how your first day back went? Okay I'm just getting ready to help John find his brother and half sister. Oh plus I called to let you know I was back in Maine.

Chapter 9

—⁓∘∾⊙⊙⋞∘∘⋟⁓—

Natasha got home and took her bag to the bedroom and started unpacking, then she went to the kitchen and decided she was going to make something fast for dinner, so she decided on spaghetti and garlic toast and a salad an he was bringing the wine. She got her sauce started, than she figured she would get the salad ready and chill it in the ice box.

Chuck got home and took a shower, out on jeans and t-shirt, listen to his answering machine, there was one message he wanted to listen to again, it said hello Detective Mooney, I heard you are looking for me, this is Jack Clark I will call you tomorrow. Chuck just couldn't believe it, so he figured he'd wait to see what he had to say tomorrow. Chuck grabbed his keys and headed out the door to go to Natasha's, first he had to stop and buy a bottle of red wine and he'd get some flowers for Natasha to wish her home.

Chuck got to Natasha's knocked on the door and she answered come on in Chuck, he handed her the wine and the flowers and gave her a kiss, thank you I love them. How does salad, spaghetti and garlic toast it sounds good, Chuck go ahead an pour us a glass of wine an lets sit and talk, so did you find out what your moms dreams were about no and she hasn't had anymore dreams and they just don't make any sense. But then you know John went to Vermont to visit his mom and when he was at his mom's she told him that his dad's name wasn't important right now because he was married and has a wife and daughter, so on the other hand we our now looking for his brother and his half sister.

Chuck says, well talking about his brother, when I got home there was a message on my answering machine and it was from Jack Clark, he is suppose to call me tomorrow, then I'll let you know what he has to say.

They sat down to eat and have more wine an talk some more about how her visit went with her mom, it went okay we did a lot of talking, trying to figure out what her dream was trying to tell us and we went out for dinner, then my coffee I went for with John, that's about all there was to it.

They got done eating there dinner and Natasha started to clean the plates up to wash them and he said I will dry and put away the dishes.

Then they sat in the living room and finished up the wine and did more talking, then Chuck said you know what this is the very first time we really spent time alone, an enjoy each others company. Chuck grabbed Natasha's hand and told her he has cared for her for so long then he reached over and kissed her and she kissed him back, they were standing up staring at each other, and then Chuck picked her up and carried her to the bedroom. Then he starts undressing her and she started undressing him then they feel on the bed, they were kissing each other, he started kissing her all over an she was going with the feeling, Chuck says here I come and he gets over the top of her and one thrust and they are both losing their minds an they are both coming to the end and they held on to each other until they were finished and he rolled off of her and she lay on his arm and they kissed each other an they went to sleep.

John woke up with a start sat up in the bed and was breathing hard trying to catch his breath, because he heard Jack calling him and saying I'm here, I'm here. He got up went to the bathroom and splashed water on his face, he then looked at the clock and he seen that it was six o'clock in the morning, so he decided he'd called down for coffee and some breakfast.

Natasha woke up laying there watching Chuck sleep, she couldn't believe the way her life was going with a man who is so caring and very understanding. So she got up and went into the bathroom to take a shower, when she got done she put on the robe an went to the kitchen to make coffee. Chuck woke up looked over an Natasha was gone, so he went into take a shower, she heard the shower running so she knew Chuck was up, so she got another cup out of the cupboard and put it next to the coffee pot. Chuck got done an got dressed in a suit he had brought with him, he went to the kitchen Natasha said your cup is on the counter by the coffee pot.

Then the phone rang an Natasha picked it up and said hello, all she heard was crying, she said mom what's the matter, I had another dream Natasha and all your dad said was he was sorry, sorry for what I don't know, I don't know what he means, okay mom take it easy and I have to get ready to go to work, so I will call you later.

Chuck said is everything all right? Yeah it was my mom saying she had another dream. I just don't know why my mom is having these dreams and they are kind of scaring her and she don't know what to do either.

CHAPTER 10

———～ω·ດ·ℓ·৩·ᘉ·ᘉ·৩·ℓ·ດ·ω———

CHUCK LEFT TO GO TO the station, he gave Natasha a kiss goodbye, Natasha said I will see you later, and please let me know what you find out from Jack.

Natasha decided she would get dressed for work and then she would call John, she went to her room put on a pantsuit and then went to the kitchen grabbed another cup of coffee and then called John he answered on the second ring hello, John I am going to the office early so if you want to come earlier that is fine.

So John finished eating his breakfast and got dressed and headed out the door so he could head to Natasha's office. He got to the office and Marie said hi John, Natasha isn't here yet, but you can wait in her office, he went in and sat down in one of the chairs in front of her desk an waited for Natasha. Natasha finally showed up and Marie said, John is waiting for you in your office. She said thanks an went in she said hi John I've got news for you, Chuck said when he got home last night he had a message on his answering machine it was from Jack, he said he heard Chuck was looking for him, he is suppose to call Chuck today an he is suppose to let me know. John said well I have to tell you something I had a dream last night about Jack all he said was I'm here, I'm here.

Natasha said, why all at once is Jack calling Chuck and coming to you in a dream, is he wanting us to find him or what.

Chuck got to the station, was sitting at his desk and his phone rang he said hello Chuck this is Jack Clark so why are you looking for me? Well I've had two robbery's here in Texas and I heard you like art, well I do like art, but I'm not that stupid, if I want art I would buy it, who told you I like art? Your brother John he hired a pi to find you, do you know this pi is there a number I can reach him at? I will give you the pi's number there probably at the office.

So Jack called Natasha's office and Marie answered hello this is Natasha Conrad pi, how may I help you, I heard my brother is looking for me and you are, Jack Clark is he there so I can talk to him, hold on, she knocked on the office door and Natasha said come in, yes Marie, there is a call for John on line one, the guy said he was your brother Jack.

John picked up the phone hello this is John, Jack where you at that's not important right now, why are you looking for me? Because you just up and vanished and me an mom didn't know where you were, oh Jack I have to tell you something that mom had told me, that our dad was married and has a daughter, so we have a half sister some where. Look John can you meet me at moms in a couple of weeks right now I've got some business to take care of and I will meet you at moms. So I don't have to look for you anymore no but we need to find our sister.

Chuck called Natasha's office and Marie said hello, Marie this is Chuck can I talk to Natasha sure hold on so she paged Natasha and she said yes, you have a call on line one

It's Chuck okay thank you. Did Jack call your office? Yeah he talked to John. Is that all you wanted yeah I will talk to you later.

John and Natasha were surprised to hear from Jack but they don't have to go looking for him, all we have to find is my sister, so can I hire you to help me find my sister, Natasha said sure, but we don't have any information about her or your dad, I mean no names.

So John told Natasha I will see you tomorrow, I'm going back to my room and call my mom. Okay I will see you tomorrow. So John went and got in his truck and headed back to his room, he got back to his room and he called his mom, his mom answered John said mom I've got good news for you, I talk to Jack and in a couple of weeks we are going to be at your house, because Jack had some business to take care of first. And I told him about our half sister.

CHAPTER 11

—⎯⎯ᴡᴡᴏᴄᴇᴛᴏᴄᴛᴇᴏᴏᴡᴡ⎯⎯—

JACK FIGURED HE WOULD TAKE the art back to the warehouse on the dock where he picked it up, he could take it back there and hope and pray that Tom Stevens shows up and gets charged for the robbery, I just got to make sure, I do not leave a print or any evidence that I've been there.

Natasha told John you are going to Vermont in a couple of weeks, so I figured I could call my mom and see what she's doing in a couple of weeks and have her go to the cabin and we could spend some more time together while you are meeting your brother and we could go buy the cabin an you could meet my mom, I'll call her first and see what she says then I'll let you know.

Oh and maybe if Chuck is done with his case he can go with us. John says Natasha I don't mean to be nosy but do you and Chuck have a thing going? Yes, Chuck was the first guy I met when I moved to Texas and I hope it turns into a big relationship so it's not just me anymore it's us.

Natasha called her mom and she said, hello mom I have a question for you, in a couple of weeks, John is coming to Vermont to talk with his brother, I wanted to know if you would like to go to Vermont in a couple of weeks so we could spend more time together. Her mom said that sounds good but I'll let you know. Then Natasha called Chuck, Chuck said hello, Natasha, Chuck what I called for John and I an maybe my mom are going to Vermont in a couple of weeks because John has to meet with Jack at his moms and I figured if you had vacation time coming you could go with us, I would like you to meet my mom, I'll let you know later when we plan on leaving. Chuck said it sounds good I'll see if I have any vacation time and let you know.

So Jack packed up all the art and loaded in his van and headed to the dock to the warehouse to drop the art off. He got to the warehouse and put the art in this little closet and left it there and took off. This was the warehouse where Tom Stevens stayed and hung out. So that way if Chuck ever found the art he wouldn't get the blame.

Natasha and John was sitting there wondering where they would start to find his sister, is your dads name on any legal papers that your mom may have, I don't know I don't think so, remember my mom wouldn't even tell me his name. Natasha said John what are you doing tonight, I thought I would call Chuck and see what he's doing and I would cook dinner tonight for us all and we could use Chucks help trying to find your sister. Sounds good to me, so she called Chuck and he said I was wondering what you are doing tonight to see if you wanted to come and join me and John for dinner tonight at my place. He said that sounds good. So Natasha told John it's on for dinner.

CHAPTER 12

—⚬〰〰⚬⊶⚬⊷⚬⊶〰〰—

LIZ CALLED NATASHA, HELLO MOM what's up I thought I'd call you to let you know I will see you in a couple of weeks at the cabin. That's good mom because hopefully Chuck can come too, because I want you to meet Chuck and John, they our very nice guy's mom but Chuck is the special man to me. Mom I would love it if we all could have dinner together, how about after he meets with his brother okay and maybe his brother can come. Okay mom I will talk to you later.

Then Chuck called Natasha hello Chuck what I called for its on for going with you and John to Vermont, my chief said that is if I wrap up my robbery case and believe me I am going to try okay I will see you later okay. Natasha called John and told him that we have two more people joining us in Vermont my mom and Chuck, but Chuck has to wrap up his case first, oh and I told my mom that I would like all of us to have dinner together and mom said maybe after you meet with Jack, that way he can come too. Natasha said, I'm going home and get ready to cook dinner, be there at 7:00 o'clock and it should be ready okay.

Jack called John on his cell phone, hello John what you doing, nothing going to dinner at 7:00 o'clock, it's nice to talk to you, Jack about our sister I don't know much about her, but I've seen dad a couple of times when we were younger and if I see a picture of him, I could identify him then me and Natasha could go from there, John I remember seeing dad too when we were younger, let me tell you something after we meet in Vermont at mom's house an hang out for awhile an get to know each other again then I will help you find our sister, well that would be nice then us four should be able to find her in no time, okay Jack I will talk to you later see you bro.

Chuck left the station to go home to get ready to go to Natasha's for dinner. But he thought he would stop off first and get some wine and flowers to take with him. He got home put the wine in the icebox and went into his room and got ready to take a shower, so he got his clothes out that he was going to wear and went an got in the shower. He got out an shaved, splash on after shave an got dressed in his jeans and t-shirt, then his phone rang he picked it up and said hello, is this detective Mooney, yes it is may I help you, no but I can help you, if you want the art that was taken go to this warehouse on the dock and you will find it, who is this? And the phone went dead. So he figured he still had a hour and a half before he had to be at Natasha's so he grabbed the flowers and wine an went out the door. He called Natasha when he got in the truck and told her Natasha I've got to go check out something first then I will be there okay.

John got ready to go to Natasha's, John said, I think I will stop and pick up a bottle of wine to take. So he stopped picked up the wine an headed for Natasha's, got there an went up to her apartment and knocked on the door, she open the door an said come in an handed her the wine and she put it in the icebox, come on lets go sit down and talk, Chuck said he had to go check something out then he would be here. You have a nice apartment Natasha yeah! I am going to have a house some day.

CHAPTER 13

⎯⎯∿⦿⦿⦿⦿⦿∿⎯⎯

CHUCK GOT TO THE WAREHOUSE an decided he would call the station on his cell phone for back up, he didn't want to enter the warehouse by himself so his back up arrived and he told the two officers I'll go in the front you go around back, if you find anyone inside you hold them. So Chuck went in with his gun drawn he looked behind ever door. Then he hit the jack pot he found the stolen art, so he shut the door back up, the two officers come in the back and poor old Tom Stevens was trying to get out. The one officer said is anybody else here, he said no just me and he asked the officers what's going on? Then Chuck showed up and said I thought you were getting rid of the art or somebody else was suppose to pick it up. What do you mean? Well Tom I found the stolen art in a closet back in the warehouse so guess what you are under arrest for having stolen property.

So Chuck asked the two officers if they would mind taking the art and Tom back to the station and he would do the paper work, because he was going to dinner.

Chuck got to Natasha's and knocked on the door and she answered the door, oh Chuck you took care of your business? Yes an guess what I got a call tonight before I left to come to your place, to tell me where I could find the art, so I had to go and check it out, an I found my missing art and I also got the guy. So I guess I am going to Vermont with you guys. Chuck said oh by the way I bought you some flowers and a bottle of wine, Natasha said John bought a bottle of wine too, so she asked Chuck to pour them some wine. So John ask Chuck so my brother wasn't involved in the robbery's Chuck said, the warehouse I checked out and found the art there was only one person there an it was Tom Stevens, there was no evidence that your brother was involved.

Jack made his anonymous call to Chuck and he would call his brother tonight and find out if the task is done. Then Jack was sitting there thinking he's got a sister and he is going to help John and Natasha found her. Jack thought I should call my mom, so he dialed the number that John gave him and she picked it up hello, hello mom this is Jack, Jack where you been me and John have been looking for you your brother hired a pi, yeah I know an this pi is going to help us find our sister, mom there looks like there's been some lies and deception, yeah Jack I'll tell you the same thing I told John I'm sorry from keeping this information from you guys okay mom we love you and we will see you in a couple of weeks.

Natasha spoke up and said dinner is ready, so they sat down and ate, then they started talking, then Natasha said well Chuck I wanted to know if you would help us find John and Jack's sister, since you are done with your case. John said we could use your help and Jack said he would help too, because we want to find our sister so she can tell us about our dad, Chuck said yes I will help you. So when are we suppose to be going to Vermont, I'm ready for a vacation, John said let me talk to Jack then I will let you guys know.

CHAPTER 14

——∿∿◦◦૨◦૭ᎧᏰᏚᎧᏰᎧ◦ᏚᎧᏰᎧᏚᎧᏚᎧᏚᎧᏰᎧ◦◦∿∿——

JOHN GOT HOME FROM NATASHA'S so he thought he would call Jack he dialed Jack's number and Jack picked up hello John what's up? Not much what I called for is everybody wants to know when we were going to Vermont, how about next weekend we can leave on Friday okay I will let everybody else know okay see you later. So John called Natasha and told her we our leaving next Friday for Vermont I just talk to Jack okay I will let Chuck know. Natasha got off the phone and told Chuck that they were leaving next Friday okay I will put in for my vacation. Chuck grabbed Natasha while he was staring at her you are so pretty and sexy, Natasha took his hand an said come with me and I will show you just how sexy I can be, they got to the bedroom an Natasha started taking off Chucks clothes and Chuck started taking off hers, Chuck picked up Natasha and layed her on the bed, he started kissing her everywhere, then she got on top of him and took over everything and he was just loving the moment, one thrust an they were lost in the moment, they reached there point of climax and she feel back on the bed, then they went to sleep.

Natasha got up the next morning and took a shower grabbed her robe and went out to make coffee then Chuck got up took a shower and got dressed and went to the kitchen to get coffee and a kiss from Natasha. Natasha said Chuck if you let me get dressed I will leave when you leave, I want to get to the office early and talk to Marie an have her set up our flights for us. So she got ready and they left. See you later. Natasha got to the office and told Marie I need you to see if you can charter a plane for next Friday for three people and we our heading to Vermont, to see if we can find John and Jack's sister an I am going to spend some time with my mom. Let me know when John comes in. Natasha called her mom and she answered the phone hello, mom I thought I'd tell you we are leaving next Friday to come to Vermont and we are trying to charter a plane, so we will, see you Friday.

So John showed up and Marie told him Natasha's in her office go in. He knocked on the door and then went in hay John I've got Marie trying to charter a plane for us that way we get there sooner.

Marie paged Natasha, she answered yes Marie I haven't had any luck chartering a plane, Natasha ask Marie if she tried Larry's Charters, well if you have luck see if we can leave at 7:00 o'clock in the morning next Friday. Marie called Larry's Charter and Larry picked it up, he said hello this is Larry's Charter, this is Marie

Adams I work for Conrad Investigations well Miss Conrad would like to know if she can charter a plane next Friday to go to Vermont at 7:00 o'clock in the morning her and two other people well Larry said let me check and see if I have a opening for next Friday, Larry looked and came back an said yes I have a opening for next Friday an we can leave when she wants okay thank you. So Marie knocked on the office door and Natasha said come in, Natasha Larry's Charter says you guys are on for next Friday okay.

So John we should get to Larry's by 6:30 in the morning next Friday so we can leave on time and we should get there by seven or eight that night, I will let Chuck know.

CHAPTER 15

⟨⟨⟨ ⟩⟩⟩

NATASHA SAID JOHN MAYBE WE can find out something about your sister while we are in Vermont, John said I hope so that way I have Jack back and I'll have my sister too. You know Natasha if you look at this whole thing there's been some lies and deception on my mom's part

Chuck went into the station and stopped at his desk and called downstairs and told them to bring up Tom Stevens so he could talk to him. So Chuck went into the room waiting for Tom to arrive, he arrived and Chuck told him to sit, I thought your boss was suppose to pick up the art, I thought he did, you didn't look in the closet to see if it was gone, no I thought it was gone, well here's how it goes now, we have no proof that there was another person in on the robbery's so I guess you and the two suspects I caught in the act all three of you are going to prison, you will be charged with receiving stolen property an trying to flee the scene. But I wasn't behind this whole thing, but we have no proof of anyone else. So Chuck got up and left the room and told the officer outside take him back downstairs.

So Chuck went back to his desk and started the paper work, sitting there thinking I'm ready for a vacation, he got done with the paper work an went into see the chief, chief I'm here to let you know I'm going to take a vacation next Friday okay, did you wrap up your case, yes sir and I even got all the art back too from both places. Chief says how long are you going to be gone I really don't know but I will let you know.

Natasha told John well I think I'm done for the day I will see you tomorrow, so John left. She called Marie in and told Marie while I'm gone to Vermont you can go ahead an take a little time off, because I don't know how long I will be gone, it all depends on if we find John and Jack's sister, I will call you.

Jack was sitting there in his room and was thinking, so Chuck must of solved his case if he was going with them to Vermont, so Jack knew he was in the clear.

Natasha got home and called her mom, mom I thought I would call you and tell you we are leaving next Friday, we should be at the cabin between seven and eight at night on Friday. I, Chuck and John would love some of that good ice tea, John's going to follow me and Chuck to the cabin to meet you and then he's leaving and going to his moms, then they our going to spend the rest of the night getting to know each other again. Then Liz said

Natasha I hope that you can help John and his brother find there sister, they seem like they really want to find her, because mom they want there sister to tell them about there dad. They only seen him a couple of times when they were younger. Okay mom I love you and I will talk to you later.

CHAPTER 16

———⟨∿∘୧⟩☙⟨୧⟩☙∿∘⟩———

LIZ SITTING AT HOME THINKING she would go to the cabin next Thursday so she could get the room ready for Natasha and her boyfriend, I can't wait to meet this Chuck, my daughter talks about him all the time.

Chuck got home and was thinking about calling Natasha to see what she was doing, so he called and Natasha was sitting on the couch watching some TV, Chuck says, I was wondering if you would like some company tonight, she said yeah sure bring that sexy body on over. So Chuck got his-self around and headed out the door to Natasha's apartment.

Jack had just got back from going out to dinner, so he figured he would call John, John picked it up an said hello, Jack said John what are you doing, I was wanting to know if I could come over and visit with you, you are in Texas yeah right now I am, yeah sure you can come an visit me, I'm staying at the hotel in town come up to room 112 okay see you later.

Chuck got to Natasha's and she let him in, so are you still watching TV, yeah she said come on we can watch together, do you want something to drink no I'm fine. Chuck says I can sure go for some dessert and Natasha says come on so she gets up and takes him by the hand and led him to the bedroom, she takes over the whole thing, throws him on the bed an starts kissing him everywhere an then starts taking off his clothes and he got up and took off hers, she threw him on the bed again and started touching him everywhere and then he threw her off of him and he took over he was touching her all over and she grabbed him around the neck and brought him down to her an she said do your magic so we both can feel good and one thrust an they were set, she was going up to meet every thrust an he did it harder and harder and they both were coming to the climax and he rolled off of her and they layed there in each others arms, Natasha says Chuck I love you I have for a long time we have come a long way and I care so much about you, then Chuck says Natasha I feel the same way about you.

Jack soon got over to John's and knocked on the door an John said come in an Jack came in an John went over and gave him a big old hug, a long time no see, I know so what have you been doing with yourself, I've been going back an forth between Texas and Vermont because I've been doing some gardening an fixing things for this women, she's very nice and she pays me good.

Then I've been in Texas taking care of some business, so what do you think about what I told you about our dad, then come to find out we have a half sister, I think its wrong of mom not to tell us his name but I think its great we found out we have a sister, John says I hope she's like this pi I hired because she's smart an very nice, I can't wait

Jack for you to meet her, then Jack asked John you aren't falling for her are you? He said no, she has a man, he's been a big help to us too, he's a detective his name is Chuck Mooney, I know him.

John I am leaving to go to Vermont tonight so you will see me next Friday at mom's house, oh by the way I called mom, and she said she was sorry for not telling us. He gave his brother a hand shake and let him out, I will see you bro.

Chuck and Natasha woke up the next morning decided they would both take a shower they would leave to go to work at the same time. While they were in the shower Chuck said, I love you too Natasha and I would like it if we could live together, she said that sounds good we will talk about it. They got out, got dressed, and went to the kitchen to make coffee, then grabbed a cup of coffee and left.

CHAPTER 17

—⟿⟾⟾⟾⟿—

NATASHA GOT UP EARLY THE next morning, thinking in two days they were going to Vermont and she figured she would get some work done. She got to the office an told Marie get us coffee an come in my office, Marie I just wanted to talk to you I want you to call Larry's an confirm my flight oh an Marie guess what Chuck told me he thinks we should move in together, so are you going too? I told him we would have to talk about it. Marie today is our last day until I come back, because tomorrow I am going to stay home an pack tomorrow then I'm going to Chuck's to spend the night at his house to help him pack, because John's going to drive to Chuck's house Friday morning then we our leaving from there, because Chuck's house is closer to Larry's Charter. John's not coming in today because I told him we would find out more about his sister when we go to Vermont.

Chuck got to the station an sat down at his desk and the Chief came to him and said, I hope you enjoy your vacation, Chuck said, I will be into work tomorrow until noon then I'm going home to pack and get other stuff in order.

Chief I don't know how long I'm going to be gone I will call you and let you know. Chief can we talk in your office it's kind of personal? Yeah, come on shut the door and Chuck sat in the chair in front of the Chief's desk, well Chief you know I've been seeing Natasha Conrad yeah, well I told her I think we should move in together, she said, we would talk about it, but see she's coming to spend the night at my house tomorrow because we our leaving from there and I was going to ask her to marry me, he said, so why are you telling me? Because I don't know if she would say yes, Chief says all you can do is try it and Chuck good luck because you guys are good together.

Liz called Natasha, Natasha answered hello mom, what's up? I was wondering if Chuck is going to stay in the same room as you, well yes mom he is, guess what mom he told me he thinks we should live together, Liz says and you told him? I told him we would talk about it, well I am happy for you Natasha, I am so happy that you have found someone to love you and that you are very happy. Liz said, I will see you in two days love you.

Marie said, Natasha if you don't mind I will stay at your apartment for you and I will get your mail for you and take care of it for you, Natasha says that sounds good I was worried about my mail, if you want you can pack your stuff and come over tomorrow before I go to Chuck's house.

Jack arrived in Vermont but went to his place, he didn't go to his mom's he figured he would go there when John came to Vermont on Friday. So he and John and there mom can sit and talk about everything going on. Hoping they could be a family again that was also including his sister if they ever find her.

CHAPTER 18

—⁓⊶⊙⟋⟍⊙⟋⟍⊙⊷⁓—

NATASHA GOT HOME GOT HER luggage out and started packing, then she went into the bathroom and got everything out of there she needed. She headed to the kitchen and decided she wanted some coffee and she would also wait for Marie to come over. Marie showed up and Natasha told her theirs coffee in the kitchen.

Natasha told Marie I think I've got everything so I'm going to get ready to go to Chuck's, okay I will see you when you get back.

Chuck got home and just sat down for a minute before he got up to start packing, he was just waiting for Natasha to show up. Then Natasha got there an knocked on his front door of his log cabin, Chuck let her in, he said, here I'll take your bags an put them over here. He said, do you want to pack first or do you want to eat, what our we having to eat, I thought we could order Chinese and while we are waiting for it we could pack then while we eat we can talk okay. They went into the bedroom and he got out his luggage, then he threw her on the bed and started kissing her then he stopped and she said, this is not getting the packing done, okay I tried, she said, you can try again later.

He got all his clothes and she put them in the suitcase, then he went to the bathroom to get everything he needed out of there, then the doorbell rang an Chuck went to answer it, then he yelled for Natasha dinner is here, so he got out two plates and two forks, he asked her what she wanted to drink, she said, you got ice tea yeah.

Well you get the ice tea and I'll bring the food in the living room they sat down and fixed there plates, he handed her plate to her an they started eating, Chuck got done eating before her and he said, well did you think about what I said about us living together, she said are you sure you want to do that, he said, if I wasn't sure I wouldn't have asked you, plus I love you Natasha and I want you to live with me, what about you love in here I have a house, maybe you can see if someone will take over your apartment.

Well Chuck if you are sure yes I will move in here and live with you, I think I have somebody to take over my place, Marie.

Then Chuck got up an dug in his pocket and then went down on one knee, an told Natasha I love you and I want you in my life forever, so please will you marry me, then Natasha didn't know what to say at first, then she said, yes I will marry you, he slipped the ring on her finger and then kissed her.

Marie called Natasha on her cell phone and told her that she would go into the office tomorrow, but after that she would be visiting her family, Natasha said, okay an Marie I have to talk to you when I get back, then Chuck said, tell her now, Marie says tell me what, I wanted to know if you wanted to take over my apartment, because I am moving in with Chuck and Marie I also wanted to know if you would be my Maiden of Honor, because we our getting married. Marie says I would be honored to stand up for you.

Natasha says Marie you can start moving your stuff in but the only thing you are going to need is your personal belongings, because I'm leaving all the furniture and everything in the kitchen, I will talk to the landlord tomorrow. Natasha thank you and Natasha I am happy for you and I am glad that you found someone, thank you Marie, I will see you when I get back and Larry said, he will be waiting for you guys in the morning and he said, when you get done in Vermont he would come back and pick you up, all you got to do is call, okay thank you.

CHAPTER 19

—⁓∿⦿⧫⦿∿⁓—

CHUCK AND NATASHA GOT UP early, Natasha went in an got a shower while Chuck went to the kitchen to make coffee, when Natasha got done then Chuck took his shower, then there was a knock on the door and she answered it hello John theirs coffee. Chuck got done and said, hello to John and he said, we will be on our way here in a few hours then will be in Vermont.

Chuck said, John can you take our bags and put them in the back of my truck, we will grab a cup of coffee to drink on the way there.

Then they left on there way to Larry's Charter, then Natasha spoke up an said, John I am moving in with Chuck plus me and Chuck are getting married, I am happy for you guys.

Okay guys we are here and there is Larry himself, Natasha got out of the truck an went an hugged Larry, she said, you guys this is a very dear friend of my dad's Larry said, well let's get the bags loaded and then we will be on our way.

So they got on there way and Larry said, it shouldn't take but a couple of hours to get there, then why did I tell my mom we wouldn't be there until 7 or 8 o'clock tonight, no its not going to take that long.

Natasha called her mom and her mom answered, hello Natasha are you guys on your way? Yes, but mom it's not going to take that long maybe a couple of hours, I thought I would call and tell you. Oh mom I am moving in with Chuck, he has a pretty log cabin, what you going to do with your apartment, I've already got someone to take over my place its Marie. Mom I will see you when I get there.

Then Natasha called her landlord, he landlord picked it up, hello this is Natasha Conrad, I thought I would call an let you know when I get back I will be moving an I have somebody that wants my place, her name is Marie Adams my secretary. Okay thank you Natasha.

Larry spoke up and said, you guys we are at the place I am going to land, Larry we have to rent cars, I took care of that already, the cars are in the hanger down there, this land and hanger are mine, okay thank you Larry. They landed got there bags and Larry took Chuck and John to the hanger to get the cars out. They took there bags and put them in the trunk of the cars. Chuck's and

Natasha's in one an John's in the other, Natasha told John you follow us to my moms, so they got on there way, they were going down the highway an Natasha says, we can tell my mom when we get there and John leaves.

Natasha said, turn here Chuck then its up the road a little ways, this is it they pulled in the driveway an Liz was waiting at the door, hello mom let's go inside, mom this is Chuck and this is John, then her mom said, John you look like my gardener, what Natasha said, he looks like my gardener his name is Clark, John said, that is my name John Clark, Natasha spoke up and said, John your twin brother Jack is my mom's gardener.

Liz says would you like some ice tea? Sure, John spoke up and told Liz my brother did this pretty flowers and the shrubs, Liz said, yes and I would like him to keep doing it for me, John said, I will let him know that.

John said, well I better get going because Jack is going to meet me at mom's house. Don't forget you and Jack are going to come here for dinner tomorrow night okay. So John left and got to his moms an Jack was sitting outside in the car waiting for John, so they both got out and there mom was waiting for them at the door, she hugged them both and told them to come in, she said, I have coffee made an they said, that sounds good, she brought the coffee to the living room and they started talking, there mom said, I am sorry for not telling you boys earlier, that's okay mom we understand, wait boys I have something else for you it's a letter your dad wrote to you, so Jack took the letter an read it out loud it said, he was sorry and not to blame your mother and I hope you find your sister love dad. We don't blame you mom, it's just a shock for both of us. Oh Jack the lady you do gardening for still wants you to be her gardener, it just so happens that it's Natasha's mom.

CHAPTER 20

—◦◦◦◦◦◦—

JACK AND JOHN GOT UP the next morning went downstairs and they went to the kitchen, there mom was fixing breakfast, she told them to sit down it was ready.

Chuck and Natasha got up and her mom was cooking breakfast too, she told them to sit we all can eat together, then Chuck said, Mrs. Conrad, call me Liz, well Liz I asked your lovely daughter to marry me an she said yes, Liz started crying an hugging both of them, then she told Chuck welcome to the family, when you guys get married, then you can come to the cabin for your honeymoon, it's nice an quiet up here, thank you mom, but we will let you know.

Natasha spoke up and told Chuck where are we going to start trying to find Jack and John's sister, then Chuck said, lets enjoy the weekend and start on Monday, we both deserve some down time. Natasha spoke up and said, mom I will help you clean up, Liz said, no you guys get dressed an you can show Chuck around the property, its going to be yours someday and I want you to enjoy it, so she kissed her mom and Chuck an said, the two most important people to me.

So they went to get dressed an went out the door hand in hand, Liz was watching them with a smile on her face.

Liz finished cleaning up and went up to take a shower, she got done an got dressed an started cleaning the whole place because they were going to have guest for dinner an she wanted the place clean. Chuck and Natasha got back an Natasha said, mom do you need help yes, you can go in the kitchen an put the salad together for me an then put some crackers and cheese on a tray for snacks until dinner is ready an Chuck you can go get me some more firewood.

They got all that done then Jack and John showed up and Chuck let them in, he told them to sit an brought them ice tea an cheese and crackers, they were all talking an then Natasha her mom an Chuck went to the kitchen, then Liz said, dinner is ready, so they all went to the kitchen an sat an ate dinner an talked.

They got done eating an Natasha got Jack and John another glass of tea an told them they could go in the living room an sit, they where going to help clean the kitchen, Jack and John were sitting there talking an John got up an started walking toward the bookcase then stopped, picked up the picture that was laying there an stared at it, then said, Jack come here, who does this look like? It looks like our dad, John called for Natasha to come in here, she said yes, John said, who is this? Oh that is my dad, John said, Natasha sit down, then Liz and Chuck came in what's going on, we asked Natasha who this is? Liz said, that's my husband, John said, Natasha this is our dad, she said what, this is our dad, then Jack said that means Natasha you are our sister.

Then Natasha said, that's what dad meant by what he told me. So mom there's been some lies and deception on dad's part.

Liz spoke up and said, I didn't know anything about this, that's why he said he was sorry. Then Liz said John do me a favor go to your mom's and bring her down here we all might as well get to know each other the past is the past.

So John left to go get his mom he got to the house an told her to come on I want to take you somewhere okay, so they left and got down to Liz's house John knocked on the door, come in they were all sitting in the living room an John told his mom to sit an he asked his mom is this my dad? And she said yes, well mom this is dad's wife Liz and his daughter Natasha the pi you hired? Yes, she is your sister? Yes. Liz said this was my idea to bring you down here. We all our family and the past is the past, I didn't know he was married until after I told him I was pregnant. Like Natasha said there has been some lies and deception.

CHAPTER 21

—⁓∙◦᠗◦᠗◦᠗⁓◦᠗∙◦⁓—

NATASHA, JOHN AND JACK WERE sitting in the kitchen at the table an she was telling them all about there dad and then Chuck walked in an told them so we need to leave Monday an go back home because they got a wedding to get ready for an he has to help Natasha to move in.

John spoke up an said, Chuck do you mind if me and Jack go back with you guys we just found our sister we don't want to let her go now, Chuck says that's fine an after you guys get married then we leave, then Liz an Meg came in the kitchen an said, when it gets close to your wedding day me and Meg will drive up together to come.

Natasha spoke up and said I am only taking my personal stuff, I don't need none of the furniture or anything in the kitchen, I will call Marie and let her know that we will be leaving Monday to come home, I will also call Larry's Charter an see if he can come Monday an take us home.

Liz spoke up an said you know, we've all went through a lot today no matter all the lies and deception we all been through we all have found each other an I don't want Meg to think I am mad at her, because I am not, I am mad at my husband, because he lied and deceived all of us.

Natasha says yeah and I got two brothers that I want to keep in touch with, an we have a sister we want to keep in touch with, Chuck spoke up an said I'm not in this family yet but I know I feel like I'm already a member of this family, but I let you all know, my main concern right now is Natasha as long as she is happy, I am happy.

Natasha said she was going to call Marie, an Marie answered hello, Marie I thought I would call you an let you know we are coming back on Monday, I thought you were helping John and Jack find their sister, I already found their sister, Marie their sister is me, I'm their sister, how did you find this out? They found a picture of my dad and they remembered what their dad looked like, then that's when they told me that was their dad too.

It's all been alright we all been talking even their mom Meg and my mom.

Natasha also said, did my landlord come over to meet you? Yes and she said we will take care of the paper work when you get back, okay I will see you later.

Liz says why don't we makes sandwiches for everybody and we can hang out for a while before we all go home. Meg says that sounds good and I will help.

Meg said, you know Liz if I knew he was married, I would have told him no, Liz says, Meg I know but lets look at it this way, my daughter has two brothers, an your sons found their sister, thank god for our children.

Liz said, sandwiches are ready and they all sat down ate and talked about family.